The Ugly Duckling

Retold by Anne Walter

Illustrated by Sarah Horne

W

FRANKLIN WATTS

LONDON•SYDNEY

First published in 2009 by
Franklin Watts
338 Euston Road
London
NW1 3BH

Franklin Watts Australia
Level 17/207 Kent Street
Sydney
NSW 2000

Text © Anne Walter 2009
Illustrations © Sarah Horne 2009

A CIP catalogue record for this book is available
from the British Library.

ISBN 978 0 7496 8538 6 (hbk)
ISBN 978 0 7496 8544 7 (pbk)

Series Editor: Melanie Palmer
Series Advisor: Dr Barrie Wade
Series Designer: Peter Scoulding

Printed in China

Franklin Watts is a division of
Hachette Children's Books,
an Hachette UK company
www.hachette.co.uk

Once upon a time, Mother Duck
sat waiting for her eggs to hatch.

The eggs soon hatched and tiny, fluffy ducklings came peeping out of the shells.

But the biggest egg still would not hatch. "Hurry up!" quacked Mother Duck, tapping the shell.

5

At last, the biggest egg hatched.
Out came a very large, very
ugly duckling.

"Oh!" said Mother Duck in
surprise. "Never mind. Now,
ducklings it's time to swim!"

Mother Duck took her ducklings to the pond. They all dived in and the large, ugly duckling was the best swimmer of all.

But because he was so ugly, all the
other birds laughed at him.

"You are too ugly to stay on this farm!" quacked one nasty duck. "Leave him alone. He can swim better than any of you!" said Mother Duck.

But the other ducks quacked and
pecked at the poor duckling.
He ran away as fast as he could.

The ugly duckling ran all the way to a marsh. There he met some geese. "What kind of bird are you?" they laughed.

The ugly duckling was sad.

"Will everybody think I'm ugly?"

he wondered.

The ugly duckling ran away again until he found a tiny cottage. He was so tired that he lay down to rest.

Next morning, he was woken
up by a clucking hen.
"Can you lay eggs?" she asked.

"No," said the ugly duckling.
"Then there is no home for you
here. Go away!" clucked the hen.

The ugly duckling ran until he
found a quiet riverbank to hide in.
One day, as he hid there,
he looked up in the sky.

He saw three beautiful white birds
flying above him. "I wish I were
like them," he thought. "Then
nobody would call me ugly."

Soon, autumn came and the leaves fell from the trees.

Then winter came. The snow fell and the river iced over. The ugly duckling was cold, hungry and very lonely.

By the time spring arrived, the ugly duckling was so lonely that he swam up the river to a pond.

On the pond were three
beautiful white birds.

"I'm going to say hello to those birds!" thought the ugly duckling, bravely. "Even if they just tell me to go away."

He took a deep breath,
looked down ...

... and saw his reflection.

"Is that me?" he gasped. He was
a beautiful white bird, too!

"What a beautiful swan you are!"
said the three white birds.
"Why don't you stay with us?"

"I'm really a swan!" said the ugly duckling, happily. And he was never called ugly again.

Puzzle 1

Put these pictures in the correct order.

Which event do you think is most important?

Now try writing the story in your own words!

Puzzle 2

Choose the correct speech bubbles for each character. Can you think of any others?
Turn over to find the answers.

Answers

Puzzle 1

The correct order is 1f, 2e, 3a, 4c, 5d, 6b.

Puzzle 2

The ugly duckling: 1, 6

Mother Duck: 2, 3

Other ducks and birds: 4, 5